Eerie Elementary

The
Science Fair is
FREAKY!

By Jack Chabert
Illustrated by Sam Ricks

BRANCHES
SCHOLASTIC INC.

READ ALL THE
Eerie Elementary
ADVENTURES!

1

2

3

4

MORE BOOKS
COMING SOON!

Table of Contents

For Sally Chabert. Thank you for always helping me
with my science homework! — JC

Text copyright © 2016 by Max Brallier
Illustrations copyright © 2016 Scholastic Inc.

Chabert, Jack, author.
The science fair is freaky! / by Jack Chabert ; illustrated by Sam Ricks. — First edition.
pages cm. — (Eerie Elementary ; 4)
Summary: For the first time in years Eerie Elementary is planning a science fair, which may not be a good idea in a school which is alive and out to get the students—but when Sam and his friends find a book of experiments that contains all of Orson Eerie's notes, it may turn out to be the key they need to finally understand the mad scientist.
ISBN 978-0-545-87368-0 (pbk. : alk. paper) — ISBN 978-0-545-87369-7 (hardcover : alk. paper) 1. Science fairs—Juvenile fiction. 2. Science projects—Juvenile fiction. 3. Elementary schools—Juvenile fiction. 4. Best friends—Juvenile fiction. 5. Scientists—Juvenile fiction. 6. Horror tales. [1. Science fairs—Fiction. 2. Science projects—Fiction. 3. Schools—Fiction. 4. Best friends—Fiction. 5. Friendship—Fiction. 6. Scientists—Fiction. 7. Horror stories.] I. Ricks, Sam, illustrator. II. Title. III. Series: Chabert, Jack. Eerie Elementary ; 4.
PZ7.C3313Se 2016
813.6—dc23 [Fic]
2015031305

ISBN 978-0-545-87369-7 (hardcover) / ISBN 978-0-545-87368-0 (paperback)

10 9 8 7 6 5 4 3 2 1   16 17 18 19 20

Printed in China   38
First edition, July 2016
Illustrated by Sam Ricks
Edited by Katie Carella
Book design by Will Denton

A BAD FEELING

Sam Graves poured baking soda into the volcano.

"Watch out!" he said.

"Get back!" Antonio cried.

"It's going to blow!" Lucy exclaimed.

But there was no reason to watch out or get back. Sam's experiment had failed miserably. Nothing blew. The volcano just sat there. Sam and his best friends, Antonio and Lucy, were studying rocks and geology in Ms. Grinker's third-grade class.

It was Monday morning, and nothing was going right for Sam. He sighed. "I stink at building baking soda volcanoes."

Ms. Grinker flicked the light switch off and on. "Class, it is time to talk about the school science fair," she said as all of the students returned to their seats. "Each student who completes a project will earn a ribbon. The fair will be held next Friday evening. You have almost two weeks to prepare."

The students chattered back and forth about what projects they might do. "Ooh, I can't wait!" Antonio said to his friends. "I'm going to do a project on snowflakes or frost. Winter is my favorite. *And* I'm pretty good at science now."

Lucy crossed her arms. "You battle *one* mad scientist and all of a sudden you think you're a science *expert*."

Orson Eerie was the mad scientist who Sam, Antonio, and Lucy had battled. He was also the architect who designed Eerie Elementary more than a hundred years ago. Orson Eerie found a way to live forever: He *became* the school. Eerie Elementary was a monster . . .

Antonio turned to Sam. "What project are you going to do?"

Just then, Sam reached into his backpack. He clutched the bright orange sash he wore whenever he was on hall monitor duty.

At first, Sam had not wanted to be Eerie Elementary's hall monitor. But, it turned out, Sam's job was much more than walking the halls. At Eerie Elementary, the hall monitor was *different*. That's because Eerie Elementary was different. Orson Eerie *was* the school — and the school was alive! It was a living, breathing thing that *fed* on students. Sam Graves, the hall monitor, was the protector of the students. Lucy and Antonio were assistant hall monitors. The three friends worked hard to keep everyone safe.

Sam clutched his hall monitor sash because he had a twisted and tangled feeling in his gut.

"Sam?" Antonio said.

"What's wrong?" Lucy asked.

As hall monitor, Sam could sense things that the other students couldn't. He could *feel* when something was wrong. And right now, Sam had that feeling.

Sam looked at his friends, and whispered, "Any second, *something* bad is going to happen. I just know it."

EARTHQUAKE!

"Quiet!" Ms. Grinker barked. The students stopped talking. "There are books in the school library to help you with your projects. Please choose a project by this Friday."

Lucy's hand shot up.

"Yes, Lucy?" Ms. Grinker asked.

"I don't remember any science fairs before this. Why is this the first time we're doing a science fair at Eerie Elementary?"

Ms. Grinker was surprised by her question. The strange feeling in Sam's stomach grew stronger as his teacher began to speak. "Well, um, Lucy, you see, last time —"

RUMBLE!
RUMBLE!

SCIENCE FAIR

The whole school began to shake! The floors trembled. The pipes clattered. Artwork on the classroom wall tumbled to the floor.

Oh no! Sam thought. *It's Orson Eerie! Something has made him mad!*

"Earthquake!" one student shouted.

"Get under your desks!" another student shouted.

Sam jumped to his feet. He watched Ms. Grinker's face turn white with fear. He had to do something.

"Everyone, remain calm!" Ms. Grinker cried as students huddled under their desks.

Sam knew this was the work of Orson Eerie. Sam would not hide. He didn't want Orson Eerie to think he was frightened.

Sam felt something tugging at his pants. He saw Lucy, looking up from beneath her desk. "Sam! What are you doing?!"

Lucy tugged again, and Sam finally got down, too.

Antonio said, "An earthquake! Can you believe it?"

Sam shook his head. "No. It's Orson Eerie. I know it . . ."

The earthquake stopped just as suddenly as it had started. No one was hurt, but everyone was spooked. When the final bell rang, the school quickly emptied.

Hall monitor duty was easy for Sam that day, because everyone was in a hurry to get home. Once the halls cleared, Sam stepped out into the cool November air. It felt *really* good to be outside.

Sam spotted Mr. Nekobi near the supply shed. Mr. Nekobi was the old man who took care of Eerie Elementary. It was Mr. Nekobi who chose Sam to be the hall monitor. He had told Sam the awful truth about the school. It was a secret shared by only Mr. Nekobi, Sam, Antonio, and Lucy.

Ms. Grinker was talking to Mr. Nekobi. Her face was bright red.

Lucy and Antonio met Sam at the rear steps.

"Lucy! Antonio!" Sam said. "Something's up. Follow me!"

The friends raced across the playground and crept behind the shed. They could hear Ms. Grinker and Mr. Nekobi's conversation.

"Ms. Grinker," Mr. Nekobi said, "it's been seven years since we held a science fair. If you recall, the last one was a disaster. You *must* cancel the fair."

"Cancel the fair?!" Ms. Grinker exclaimed. "Impossible! I've already sent invitations to all the parents!"

"But you *must* remember," Mr. Nekobi warned. "There was an earthquake just days before that science fair, too. I'm afraid *this* science fair might bring the same kind of trouble . . . *Dangerous* trouble."

"Today's quake was simply a coincidence. After all, *what else* could it be?" Ms. Grinker said as she turned and walked away.

Sam could not believe what he had just heard. He turned to his friends. "I'm afraid this science fair is a bad idea," Sam said. He swallowed hard.

SNATCHED!

3

The next morning, Sam, Antonio, and Lucy were at the school library. They had arrived extra early and no one else was around. The bookshelves loomed over the friends as they walked through the long stacks.

"*Ahhh-choo!*" Lucy sneezed for the ninth time in the past three minutes. "This must be the dustiest library in the world." She scrunched up her face to fight off another sneeze.

"Most of these books are older than Mr. Nekobi!" Antonio joked.

"I'm not sure *anything* is older than Mr. Nekobi!" Sam said.

Sam was making a joke, but inside he felt nervous. The earthquake had been strange. And what Mr. Nekobi had *said* was even stranger: There was an earthquake just before the last science fair, too? *What did Mr. Nekobi mean when he said the last science fair had been "a disaster"? Had the school attacked the students?*

The friends found the science section. There were dozens and dozens of books. Sam reached up to take one, but there was a loud —

SNAP!

"Whoa!" Antonio exclaimed. He had stepped right through an old, worn-out heating vent in the floor. "Wait a minute!" The vent cracked more as he pulled his foot free. "There's something in here . . ."

Antonio got down on the floor for a closer look. He reached into the dark vent.

Suddenly, Antonio's eyes burst wide open. "It's got me!" he shrieked. "Something's got my hand! Help!"

A STRANGE DISCOVERY

Sam and Lucy watched in horror. Something inside the vent had hold of Antonio. Sam was about to grab him when Antonio flashed a big grin.

"Just teasing!" Antonio said. "I got you guys *good*!"

Lucy threw her hands up in the air. "You scared us!"

"There *is* something down here, though,"
Antonio said as he felt around inside the vent.
He pulled out a book.

"Weird," Sam said.

Antonio got to his feet and held up the
book. It was covered in a layer of dust an inch
thick. "Why would this be in the vent?"

Sam and Lucy stepped closer. The book
looked *ancient*. It looked one hundred years
old, at least. Lucy's eyes scrunched up tight
and —

"AHH-CHOO!"

Lucy sneezed again, blowing the thick
layer of dust into the air.

The friends could see the book cover now:

The old book's pages seemed to crack as Antonio opened it. The smell of wet dog and damp basement spilled from the book.

Suddenly, Sam had that feeling in his stomach again. The feeling that something bad was going to happen.

"Look!" Lucy said, pointing. There was handwriting on the first page of the book. The writing looked very old-fashioned and fancy.

The friends leaned closer and squinted. But before they could make out the strange writing... **FWOOOM!** The book leapt from Antonio's hands! It shot up into the air!

The friends jumped back. The book flapped open and closed. Dust showered them. The book bobbed twice in the air, then began *zipping* down the dark stacks.

"It's flying!" Sam exclaimed.

"Orson Eerie must be controlling it," Antonio said, huddling close to Sam and Lucy. "Books *normally* don't fly."

"Nothing in this school is normal," Lucy replied.

In an instant, Sam knew that this book was *important*. For some reason, Orson Eerie didn't want them getting their hands on it.

"Guys!" Sam shouted. "Don't let that book get away!"

GET THAT BOOK!

5

Sam and his friends chased after the flying book. The lights in the library flickered, then blinked off completely.

The library was almost pitch-black now. Computer monitors glowed dimly in the corner. They gave off the only light in the room. The entire library had a spooky feel. It felt like something might jump out from the darkness.

Sam, Antonio, and Lucy began to creep through the shadowy stacks. They were no longer sure if they were chasing the book, or if the book was chasing them.

Sam crept around the corner and —

WHOOSH!

The book zoomed toward him! It opened and closed, like a dark crow flapping its wings. Sam leapt, reaching for the book like he was trying to catch a line drive in Little League.

But the book soared higher, then zoomed left.

Sam saw the open library door. "It's headed for the door! Don't let it escape!" he shouted.

"I'll handle it!" Lucy said.

Lucy sprinted across the library. She threw her body against the door, slamming it shut.

An instant later, the book banged into the door. It fluttered a moment, then swooped left. It disappeared into the darkness.

"Orson Eerie must *really* not want us to read that book," Sam whispered.

"With the door shut, it's trapped in here," Antonio said. "Right?"

Is there any other way for it to escape?
Lucy asked.

At once, they cried, "The broken vent!"

Sam and his friends darted through the stacks. Books leapt from the shelves! One slammed into Sam's stomach, knocking him to the side. Another clonked Antonio in the shoulder. Lucy ducked just before an encyclopedia took her head off.

As Sam raced toward the vent, one book hung in the air. It was a massive dictionary. Sam tried to slide beneath it, but —

KA-POOF!

The dictionary exploded! Scraps and strips of white paper filled the air like a winter blizzard.

Sam couldn't see a thing, but he raced forward anyway. He pushed through the paper-filled air. Sam kept his eyes shut. *I don't want to get a paper-cut on my eyeball!* he thought.

Even though Sam couldn't see, he *sensed* that he was close to the book. It was within reach. He dove, with his arms out and his hands open! He felt something touch his palms. He shut his fingers tightly and fell to the floor with a heavy OOMPH.

"Nice grab!" Antonio said.

Sam opened his eyes. He was clenching the book in his hands.

Instantly, the lights flickered back on. With a loud **BANG**, **SLAM**, and **POW** all the other books crashed to the floor.

Everything was silent.

"Now," Sam said, "let's have a look at this book . . ."

THE MYSTERY
OF THE BOOK

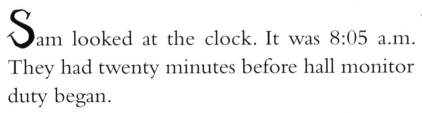

Sam looked at the clock. It was 8:05 a.m. They had twenty minutes before hall monitor duty began.

"Do you think the book will fly away again?" Antonio asked.

"No," Sam said. "I think the chase drained the school's energy. At least for now."

Sam opened the book to the first page. The friends leaned closer to read the handwritten words inside:

I donate this book to the school I designed. This was my favorite science book as a child. It inspired me for many years. Maybe someday it will inspire the students of Eerie Elementary.

Signed,
Orson Eerie

Sam's heart began to pound. "This book was given to the school by Orson Eerie!" he said. "This book *belonged* to Orson Eerie!"

KLANG! The friends jumped as the door banged open. Mr. Nekobi rushed in. "I heard strange noises," he said.

"Mr. Nekobi!" Sam exclaimed. "You have to see this!"

Sam pushed the ancient book across the table. Mr. Nekobi took a deep breath. "*Strange Science Experiments to Dazzle and Amaze,*" he said, reading the title aloud. "I haven't seen this book in years . . ."

"It used to belong to Orson Eerie!" Sam said.

Mr. Nekobi sighed deeply. "I know. A student used it to find a project for the last science fair, seven years ago."

"We heard the last fair was a disaster. What happened?" Lucy asked. "Was Eerie Elementary trying to feed on the students?"

"No," Mr. Nekobi said. "That's what was so strange. The school just began *destroying* things. It was a miracle no one was hurt. There was only *one* thing missing when the fair ended."

"What?" Sam asked.

Mr. Nekobi handed the book back to Sam. In a very serious tone he said, "This book."

Just like that, Mr. Nekobi turned away. He began cleaning up the scattered books.

Sam ran his hand through his hair. He thought and thought, but he couldn't make sense of Orson Eerie's note. "So we know Orson donated this book," Sam said. "But why doesn't he want us to have it? What's in here that he doesn't want us to see?"

"And why was there a weird *earthquake* yesterday?" Antonio added.

"Was the earthquake a warning from Orson?" Lucy wondered. "A warning that the science fair shouldn't happen?"

"Maybe," Sam replied. "But this doesn't feel like the other times we've battled Orson. This feels different." He looked down at the book. "There must be something in here . . . Something Orson Eerie doesn't want *anyone* to read. *Ever.* We just need to find out what it is."

SAM'S BIG CHOICE

7

Over the next few days, Sam and his friends read *Strange Science Experiments to Dazzle and Amaze* from cover to cover. They searched every inch of every page. They hunted for hidden messages or secret notes.

But there was nothing. They saw nothing that would explain *why* Orson Eerie would want this book all to himself.

"Coming guys!" Sam shouted. It was Friday morning and Antonio and Lucy were outside Sam's house. They were waiting for him so they could all walk to school together.

"Happy Friday, buddy!" Antonio said.

Sam stopped in his tracks. "Oh no! I totally forgot! It's Friday!" Sam exclaimed. "Today is the day we have to tell Ms. Grinker what projects we're doing!"

Lucy and Antonio looked at each other. "Um," Lucy said. "But the only science book we borrowed from the library is *Strange Science Experiments to Dazzle and Amaze . . .*"

"We'll have to choose our projects from that book," Antonio said.

I'm not sure this is the best idea, thought Sam. But it was the only choice. Sam knew Ms. Grinker would ask for their choices as soon as class began. He hung his head and trudged back inside. Moments later, he returned with the book. The friends took a seat on the front steps and Antonio carefully turned the book's crinkly pages.

"I'll do this one!" Antonio said, pointing to "Weather Wonders: Hot and Cold."

He turned the pages. Lucy's eyes lit up when she saw a project titled "Making Invisible Ink with Lemon Juice." "I'm doing that!" Lucy said.

Antonio groaned. "Aw, man! Invisible ink! That's awesome spy stuff!"

Lucy laughed. "It's mine now!"

"Well, Sam," Antonio said. "What project will you pick?" He passed the book to Sam.

Sam didn't respond. He was focused on the ancient, yellowed pages. *I can't believe I'm reading the same book that Orson Eerie read*, Sam thought. *My fingers are turning the same pages that Orson's fingers turned, over one hundred years ago.*

Sam hated holding the book. It felt like Orson Eerie was reading over his shoulder. The feeling made Sam's skin crawl.

A single experiment caught Sam's eye. It was circled in faded pen and there was a star next to it:

"This is the project I messed up in class last week," Sam said.

Lucy pointed to the star. "It looks like it was Orson's favorite."

Sam wondered what would happen if he performed Orson Eerie's favorite project *at* Eerie Elementary. It didn't sound like the note on the first page of the book had been written by a crazy mad scientist. Maybe Orson Eerie hadn't *always* been evil? Maybe Orson Eerie would be happy to see someone using his favorite book?

Sam clapped the book shut. "I'll do it. I'll do the 'Baking Soda Volcano.'"

With that, Sam placed the book back inside his house. He wouldn't bring the book to Eerie Elementary. He couldn't risk the school stealing it back.

As Sam and his friends walked to school, Sam kept thinking about the experiment. He chose the baking soda volcano project because he wanted to prove to himself that he could do it. But he also chose it because he hoped it would give him a chance to please Orson Eerie — and keep everyone safe. Sam just had to get the experiment right this time . . .

THE SCIENCE FAIR BEGINS

For a full week, the friends worked on their projects. Lucy was soon a master in writing with homemade invisible ink. Antonio knew everything there was to know about heat, frost, and snow.

But Sam's project never worked! Every time, Sam made a mistake. He wondered if, maybe, Orson Eerie was *causing* him to fail.

Soon it was Friday night: the evening of the science fair. The school gymnasium was packed.

TAP! TAP! TAP! Ms. Grinker stood at the front of the gym, tapping on the microphone. She called for attention, then thanked the parents, students, and teachers for coming.

"Welcome to the science fair," she said. "I'll be walking around to judge the projects . . ."

While Ms. Grinker spoke, parents and teachers walked the maze of tables. Sam and his friends stood by their projects. Sam looked over at Lucy and Antonio. Like Sam, they were nervously waiting for something to happen.

Sam saw his mom walking toward him. That made him feel just a bit better. But then he saw what was in her hand . . .

It was the book! *Strange Science Experiments to Dazzle and Amaze*!

Suddenly, Sam felt hot and light-headed. He began to sweat.

"Sam, I thought you might need this," his mom said as she handed him the book. Sam took it with trembling hands.

"Um, um . . . ," Sam said. He couldn't form any words.

"Are you okay?" his mom asked.

Sam nodded. "Uh, yeah, Mom. I'm fine."

Sam's mom smiled and rustled his hair. "That's some volcano!" she said as she turned to leave. "Looks ready to blow!"

Sam tried to smile, but his heart was pounding. His mom had brought the book *to the school*! That was the worst thing possible! Orson Eerie would know it was here. He would *sense* it.

Sam quickly jammed the book inside his backpack. He zipped his bag shut tight. But just as he did, it began to shake . . .

Oh no, Sam thought.

"Lucy, what do we have here?" Ms. Grinker asked as she stood over Lucy's project.

Sam looked up. Lucy dipped a Q-tip into a bowl of lemon juice and wrote on a piece of paper. The juice dried, and the message became invisible.

While Lucy was performing her science experiment, Sam's backpack banged against the table leg. The book was trying to escape! Sam coughed to cover the sound.

"Now watch," Lucy said to Ms. Grinker. "When I heat the paper with this flashlight, you will be able to read what I wrote. See?"

Ms. Grinker chuckled. "You earn a ribbon," she said.

The zipper on Sam's backpack began to move on its own. To Sam, the sound of the zipper was as loud as crackling thunder.

"Antonio," Ms. Grinker said, "you may begin your project."

Antonio started talking, but Sam could hardly pay attention.

"Lucy," Sam whispered as he grabbed his backpack and zipped it up. "Cover for me."

Lucy looked at Sam, confused. "Where are you going?"

"Away from here!" Sam said. "My mom brought the book! I shoved it in my backpack, but the book is coming to life! Orson must be calling it!"

"We have to get it out of here!" Lucy exclaimed.

But before Sam could respond, he saw Ms. Grinker standing in front of him — staring at him. "Going somewhere, Mr. Graves?" she asked.

Sam stuttered. "Um, ah, I was just —"

"Just about to present your project, I hope," Ms. Grinker said. "It's your turn."

Sam gulped, set the backpack down on the floor, and began his experiment.

Sam began to perform his project. The first step was pouring dish soap into the volcano. Sam reached for the dish soap bottle. But somehow, the top popped off and soap burst out. Ms. Grinker frowned.

I didn't even touch it, Sam thought.

ZiPPPP!

Sam looked down at his backpack. It was opening again.

Oh no, Sam realized. *Orson is messing up my project to distract me. That way, he can take back the book without me being able to stop him!*

Sam stomped on his backpack. His sneaker pressed the zipper against the gym floor.

Antonio rushed to wipe up the dish soap. "There you go, buddy," he said.

Sam smiled weakly and again reached for the soap. It nearly erupted a second time, but Sam quickly placed his hand over the top of the bottle. Then he poured some soap into the volcano.

Phew.

Next was the baking soda and the orange food coloring. As Sam reached for the baking soda, it toppled over — on its own! Sam hadn't even touched it! This time, Lucy stepped over to help clean up the mess.

"Lucy," Ms. Grinker said, "please let Sam finish his project himself."

Lucy slunk back to her own table.

Sam pressed his foot harder against the backpack zipper. It continued to try to worm its way out from beneath his sneaker.

He could feel Ms. Grinker watching him. He poured the baking soda and some food coloring into the top of the volcano.

"Now," Sam announced, "in one moment, I will pour in the vinegar. This last ingredient will cause the volcano to erupt."

As Sam said those words, he felt the zipper squirm out from beneath his foot. His eyes shot to the floor.

The backpack was open! And it was empty!

UH-OH . . .

10

Antonio spotted Orson Eerie's mysterious book sliding across the floor. His eyes grew wide. The book was closest to Lucy. She dove behind Sam's science fair table. Sam tried to watch as Lucy grabbed hold of the book. But Ms. Grinker was telling him to hurry up and complete his project.

The book tried to wrestle free from Lucy's hands, but Lucy fought back. She squeezed the book and was able to stuff it inside Sam's backpack. She zipped the backpack shut and jammed it beneath Sam's foot. She popped up from behind the table.

Ms. Grinker glared at her.

"Sorry!" Lucy said. "I just thought I saw a — um — penny on the floor!"

Ms. Grinker turned back to Sam as he slowly poured the vinegar into the top of the volcano.

"Now my volcano will erupt!" Sam said. "I mean, it *should* erupt."

Sam held his breath. After a moment, the soap, baking soda, and vinegar mixture came rushing down the side.

Ms. Grinker smiled. "Well, that wasn't the *smoothest* experiment I've seen tonight, but it was successful. Nice job, Sam! You earn a ribbon."

For a brief moment, Sam felt proud. He had done it! His experiment had worked!

But then he had that sinking feeling — the feeling that something *bad* was going to happen. An instant later, it did . . .

Sam stumbled as he felt the backpack slip out from beneath his foot. It was escaping! All of a sudden, it was chaos at the fair!

Science projects began reacting strangely. Eggs cracked, soda bottles burst, and smoke filled the air! Parents gasped. Teachers cried out. Students ran for cover. "Oh no! Not again!" Ms. Grinker shrieked.

Ms. Grinker hurried for the exit, pulling students with her as she ran. Mr. Nekobi quickly led everyone else outside.

KA-BOOM! A project exploded behind Sam. "Watch out!" Lucy said. She grabbed Sam and Antonio and yanked them both toward the door.

"Let's get out of here!" Antonio yelled.

The Big Bang Theory

Why Do Things Explode?

Sam slid to a stop on the slippery floor. "Not without the book!" he said. "Orson is doing *all of this* to get his book back. It MUST be important!"

"I put the book in your backpack . . ." said Lucy.

". . . which was under my foot a minute ago," added Sam.

Antonio looked out at the chaos. "But where is it *now*?!" he cried.

THE SCIENCE FAIR DISASTER

11

Water poured down like in a hurricane! Smoke from a student's battery project had caused the sprinkler system to turn on.

Sam and his friends stared out at the huge
room. It was madness! The lights flickered
and the walls moaned. The floor rumbled
and the bleachers howled. A chill ran down
Sam's spine.

"We have to find my backpack," Sam said. "The book is in there!"

He rushed over to his project. The volcano was flipped onto its side. He peeked over it.

Sam smiled as he saw his backpack behind the table. But it was unzipped again. "No!" he cried, grabbing the backpack.

The book was gone.

"Find that book!" Sam yelled.

The friends searched the room. Their eyes looked over everything, but it was hard to see. Smoke filled the air. Water dripped from the sprinklers. Experiments bubbled over. There were big *popping* sounds and small *snapping* explosions.

"There!" Lucy finally exclaimed, pointing. They all saw it. And they all gasped . . .

The book was sliding across the gym floor, toward the center of the room. It was being moved by the power of Eerie Elementary.

Sam charged toward the book. "Come on, guys!"

As they ran, the ground began to tremble and shake.

"Another earthquake?!" Antonio shrieked.

The large wooden floorboards began to shift. The floor started to split apart. Pipes and wires burst from below.

"This is no earthquake!" Sam shouted. "It's a volcano!"

VOLCANO!

12

A giant volcano was rising up from the gymnasium floor. It was a volcano built of floorboards and metal pipes and old brick. A blast of heat sent Sam and his friends stumbling back.

"There's a volcano . . ." Antonio said, eyes wide. "A *real* volcano. Inside the gym!"

Sam kept his eyes on the book. It was near the mouth of the volcano: the crater. As the volcano continued to grow taller, the book was raised higher into the air. Every second it moved farther from Sam's grasp.

Soon the volcano was completely formed. The book rested on the edge of the crater.

A sudden, tremendous **BURP** sound echoed through the gym. Lava began splashing and spitting from the mouth of the volcano.

Sam's heart started to pound.

The lava was made from the materials in his experiment: dish soap, baking soda, food coloring, and vinegar. But it was boiling and red-hot.

Cracks formed at Sam's feet. Lucy and Antonio jumped back as lava began to bubble up from the floor.

"We need to climb the volcano! We need to reach that book!" Sam said.

"How do we fight a volcano?" Lucy cried.

Sam's eyes darted across the gym. Hanging near each doorway was a fire extinguisher. There were three in total. "Grab those!" Sam yelled to his friends.

Moments later, they had each lifted the heavy fire extinguishers into their backpacks. Then, using all their might, they slipped their backpacks over their shoulders. They grabbed the nozzles and held them, ready to fire.

Lucy squeezed the spray nozzle to test it. A stream of white foam burst out.

"That stuff looks like marshmallow fluff!" Antonio said.

Sam spotted his hall monitor sash. It had fallen from his backpack during the chaos. He plucked it from the ground and slung it over his shoulder.

Lava was rushing from the floor. Soon, it would overtake them.

He looked to his friends and said, "Fire!"

FIREFIGHTERS

13

Sam, Lucy, and Antonio shot their fire extinguishers at the floor as lava bubbled up at their feet. The hot lava hissed and cooled as they blasted it.

"The marshmallow fluff stuff is working!" Lucy exclaimed.

"You guys take care of the lava coming from these cracks," Sam said. "I'm going to get the book."

Sam charged up the side of the volcano before his friends could stop him. But it soon became a struggle to climb . . .

Lava bubbled from the volcano's crater. The floorboards that formed the volcano were melting! Sam's heart pounded. It felt like his shoes were melting! One floorboard disappeared at his feet, and he leapt to the next. He had to jump from floorboard to floorboard before they turned to lava.

The same thing was happening down below. Antonio and Lucy jumped from one floorboard to another. "It's like we're playing the 'floor is lava' game," Antonio said.

"This is no game!" Lucy barked. "Watch out behind you!"

"Oh yeah!" Antonio said. He spun around and sprayed the oozing lava at their feet.

Sam eyed the book. It was perched on the crater. As the lava spit and the volcano shook, the book wobbled. It was about to fall in. If Sam didn't hurry, the book would be lost forever! Orson Eerie was about to swallow it up!

Sam gripped a piece of warm metal pipe and pulled himself up.

The volcano was at least thirty feet high. Sam panted as he reached the peak.

The volcano heaved and shook. The book rocked back and forth on the lip of the crater, and then —

It tumbled over the side, into the volcano!

"No!" Sam shouted. He lunged forward and jammed his hand into the mouth of the volcano. He snatched it at the last moment! The book was as hot as fire. But he held it in his hand.

He yanked his hand out of the crater and stumbled back.

ROOOARRR!

The volcano began to shake. Sam peered down into the hot mouth of the volcano. Lava was bubbling and splashing and rising!

This giant volcano — the volcano that IS Orson Eerie — is furious! It lost the book again. And it won't stop until it gets it back! Sam thought.

Lucy exclaimed, "Sam! That volcano is going to blow!"

THE FACE OF ORSON EERIE

Flaming-hot lava bubbled and splashed at the top of the volcano. Sam shouted down to his friends. "Guys! I need backup!"

Lucy and Antonio began scrambling up the volcano. Suddenly, it erupted! Lava streamed down the side.

"Follow Sam's path!" Lucy shouted as she darted past a sizzling pipe.

"I'm trying!" Antonio said as he jumped over a stream of lava. They jumped from one safe spot to the next, until they were at the top. There, they were able to steady themselves.

"Everyone! Fire into the volcano!" Sam shouted.

Together, the three friends aimed their fire extinguisher nozzles and sprayed.

The lava became covered in white foam. Steam poured off the lava. The volcano shook. The lights flashed on and off. It felt like the entire gymnasium was about to crumble around them.

Finally, the volcano shifted and rocked. It was beginning to sink back into the ground.

"It's working!" Lucy said. "We're like *real* firefighters!"

"Or *volcano fighters*!" Antonio shouted, smiling. "Right, Sam?"

But Sam didn't hear his friends. He was too busy staring into the bubbling lava. Sam saw something.

A face.

The face of Orson Eerie.

And it was staring right back at Sam. The face seemed to be telling Sam that someday, he would fail. It was telling Sam that he could not protect the school forever.

Even though the room was hot, Sam felt a chill rush through his body.

"What is it, Sam?" Lucy asked.

Sam stared back at the red-hot face. "Aim at the center of the lava! NOW!" he ordered.

At once, the three friends blasted the spot where Sam had, for a brief moment, seen the face of Orson Eerie.

VOOOSH!

The volcano swayed from side to side. The floorboards and pipes sunk into the floor.

Just as the fire extinguishers were nearly empty, the volcano was gone. The floorboards settled into place. The gym floor returned to normal. Sam, Lucy, and Antonio were back on solid ground. Smoke hung in the air.

Antonio wiped the sweat from his brow.

But then —
SLAM!

MYSTERY SOLVED

The doors flew open! Parents, teachers, and students rushed into the gymnasium. They all looked terrified. The gym was a complete disaster. Broken science projects covered the floor. White foam dripped from everything.

"Sam!" his mom cried out.

"Lucy!" her parents yelled.

"Antonio!" his father shouted.

The three friends were standing in the middle of the gym. Their parents relaxed when they saw that they were safe.

Sam's mom spotted the fire extinguishers. "Did you put out a fire?" she exclaimed.

Sam shrugged. "Sort of."

"It was just a small one," Lucy added, trying to keep their secret safe.

"Super tiny. Barely anything!" Antonio said with a smile.

Ms. Grinker ran her fingers through her thin, gray hair. She muttered, "We are *never* having another science fair."

The parents and teachers all agreed the science fair had been awful. But the students thought it was pretty fantastic.

Sam, Lucy, and Antonio walked toward the parking lot. As they stepped off the school grounds, Sam pulled Orson Eerie's book from his backpack. "Whoa!" he said. "It's still hot!"

All of a sudden, Lucy's eyes lit up — like a lightbulb had gone off in her head. "Let me see that!" she cried.

She yanked the book from Sam's hands and flipped it open. "Look, guys!" she exclaimed. "There's writing on these pages!"

"Huh?" Sam asked. "What do you mean?"

"Yeah. We already looked and didn't find anything. You know that," Antonio added.

"My invisible ink project!" Lucy said. "I found that project in *this* book! And look — Orson wrote notes in here *in invisible ink*!"

Sam and Antonio both leaned in to get a closer look.

Lucy said, "The heat from the lava made the invisible writing readable — just like how it worked in my project!"

She flipped through the pages of the book. There was writing on all of them. Hundreds and hundreds of words, and it was *all* in Orson Eerie's fancy, old-fashioned handwriting.

"That's why Orson was trying so hard to get the book back," Antonio said. "It contains his secrets!"

"It will take us forever to go through all of these notes," said Lucy. "And it looks like Orson may have written some of these notes in code."

Sam was silent. He knew this book was important. He knew it could be the key to understanding how Orson Eerie became a mad scientist. It could be the key to *everything*.

Sam finally spoke up. "Maybe, just maybe, this book will show us how to stop Eerie Elementary once and for all . . ."

Shhhh!

This news is top secret:

Jack Chabert is a pen name for Max Brallier. (Max uses a made-up name instead of his real name so Orson Eerie won't come after him, too!)

Max was once a hall monitor at Joshua Eaton Elementary School in Reading, MA. But today, Max lives in a weird, old apartment building in New York City. His days are spent writing, playing video games, and reading comic books. And at night, he walks the halls, always prepared for the moment when his building will come alive.

Max is the author of more than twenty books for children, including the middle-grade series The Last Kids on Earth and Galactic Hot Dogs.

Sam Ricks went to a haunted elementary school, but he never got to be the hall monitor. As far as Sam knows, the school never tried to eat him. Sam graduated from The University of Baltimore with a master's degree in design. During the day, he illustrates from the comfort of his non-carnivorous home. And at night, he reads strange tales to his four children.

HOW MUCH DO YOU KNOW ABOUT

Eerie Elementary

The Science Fair is FREAKY?

Why does Mr. Nekobi think the school science fair should be cancelled?

Why does Sam choose to do the baking soda volcano experiment?

What is happening in the picture on page 57?

How do Sam, Antonio, and Lucy defeat the volcano?

Which science fair project would **you** choose: the volcano, the invisible ink, or the weather? Write one paragraph explaining your opinion. Then research how to do the project!